Diva Las Vegas

Russ T. Hammer

To order additional copies of this book, contact:
Xlibris
844-714-8691
www.Xlibris.com
Orders@Xlibris.com

ISBN: Softcover   979-8-3694-1335-7
        EBook   979-8-3694-1334-0

Print information available on the last page

Rev. date: 12/27/2023

well girls, here is my opinion on Relationships; Friendships & Healthy Romantic Partners. I call it BISCUITS AND CAKES

A friendship, like a relationship is always two sided both people need to be seeking a friendship. A one-sided interest is an attempt at friendship, where a relationship will never work.

A solid relationship needs communication. honesty, respect, and trust or it's not real.

The best of friendships are usually with the people you've had a relationship with the longest, because of quality time, bonding time, and experiences shared together. The recipe for a good friendship is like a recipe for making biscuits.

BISCUITS		FRIENDSHIP
Flour	=	Communication
Baking Powder	=	Honesty/Fairness
Milk	=	Respect/Empathy
Eggs	=	Integrity
Salt	=	Trust/Compassion
Butter	=	Similar Interests
Kneed-Dough	=	Quality Time
Bake	=	Deep bonding Friendships

The recipe for a healthy romantic relationship is like making a cake. If any of the ingredients are missing or if short cuts are taken, the cake will be ruined. You must take your time to have the perfect cake.

CAKE		ROMANTIC RELATIONSHIP
Flour	=	Communication
Baking Powder	=	Honesty/Fairness
Milk	=	Respect/Empathy
Eggs	=	Integrity
Salt	=	Trust/Compassion
Cooking Oil	=	Similar Interests
Flavoring	=	Attraction
Sugar	=	Romance
Mix in Bowl	=	Quality time
Bake	=	Deep feelings/Love
Let Cool	=	Emotional Intimacy
Frost	=	Make Love
		(Physical Intimacy = Sex)

Note that the first six ingredients in both relationship-recipes are nearly the same, because it Is possible to have a good healthy friendship with a member of the opposite sex.

The unhealthy decision most people make (in the pursuit of a romantic relationship is becoming intimate to soon!) frosting the cake before it's cooked and allowed to cool! Skipping some or most of the important key ingredients.

Example: You meet a person you're really attracted to. Later (later that night or within a few days, you end up engaging in physical intimacy (sex.) You've frosted an un-prepared cake.

(In reality, It's not even a cake yet!) You've gone from little communication, to attraction, to sex. Most of the key ingredients are missing. The relationship may last for a while but will most likely fail because you are missing better communication, honesty, fairness, respect, integrity, trust, compassion, similar interests, romance, quality time, time to bond, and time to truly fall in love.

Frosting alone is fun, but it's unhealthy!

It's easy to love the frosting, but never frost the cake before it's truly a cake! If you frost a cake before it's ready, all you have is a big mess. Remember, you can't un-frost a cake. Imagine trying to frost a bowl of flour, baking powder, milk, eggs, salt, cooking oil that's mixed in a bowl, but not baked or cooked. You can imagine the mess. In a relationship you can't physically see the mess, but your emotions are as mixed as the ingredients in the bowl. Confusing and unidentifiable. (x 2 for each of the people involved.) Remember you CAN'T un-frost a cake. When relationships are given time to mature, they'll always be better, more fulfilling, and more stable.

A biscuit pan usually has six to twelve places to put the dough (for baking biscuits,) because a person can have many friends. A cake pan only has one place for a cake and the ingredients, because in a health, strong and stable romantic relationship it's better when you're only involved in one. Otherwise, there's no long-term success for many reasons. **An <u>emotionally painful</u> break-up is inevitable.**

A person involved in many physical intimate relationships may nave many cupcakes, but none are as meaningful and fulfilling as a **true Healthy Romantic Relationship**. And later in life, He or She will more than likely regret never experiencing, "the Perfect Cake!" (**Having the Love of their Life**!)

This is how I define "Real Love," There's a stunning connection that occurs when you meet your perfect mate. The discovery of each other is intoxicating. The unusual spectrum of dynamic emotions is an unmistakable attraction, so much more than merely physical. This deep emotional connection magnified by an almost spiritual awareness changes the ordinary into the unimaginable. People instinctively seek this type of companionship hoping to discover that entrancing person that completes, compliments, and fulfills that part of them that doesn't exist in the presents of anyone else. Like Adam searching for his missing rib and the perfect rib yearning to belong, the two intricately weave the missing parts of each other. Emotionally, intellectually, Psychologically and some how chemically. As if their hearts seem to speak to each other before a single word is ever spoken. This sincere recognition of all these sensations simultaneously is true love. Amazingly this profound electric connection is experienced long before any physical passion is even considered or imagined. This eclectic magnetism conquers all mind, body, spirit. The kind of love lasts a lifetime and is literally perpetual between the couple. Once experienced, it's never forgotten and forever unequalled in the feelings for anyone else. This uncompromising feeling of attraction is not settling for someone you can learn to live with and develop feelings for, it's finding that entrancing person you never knew you needed and now realize you can't live without!

Anyway, that's what I think. Say's BOB. Cool! We've landed in Las Vegas...

Where's my Jacket?

Major we're in Las Vegas, you don't
Need a jacket!

If the Temperature is Lower than my Age,
I need My jacket!

But Major, You're 92!

Bob and the Major
Play Blackjack
With twin sisters,
Ima & Inna Pickle...

10

Bob takes the Major to "The MGM Grand,"
To see the Forgotten Fountains!

BOB thought this was "The Miss America Contest" But,
It was a contest for fancy spray bottles...

14

Major, we need to go…

What time is it?

It's 3:00…

But I just started Playing after Lunch…

Yes, Major but, it's 3:00

In the morning?

I don't want to Stop yet, I'm Winning!

How much have you Won?

I'm ahead 45 Cents!

BOB won a motorcycle but, doesn't know how to ride it. Later, at "Counts Kustoms," BOB got Danny and the guys to add Training Wheels...

Danny didn't want too, but later said, "It was worth it, just to see the Smile on his Face!"

Happy Birthday Major !!

It's important to remember, you can accomplish anything if you just believe in yourself, you are an amazing individual. We only have one chance at life (Unless you're a butterfly or a Jelly fish)

Be all the you, you can be. We will never be perfect, but don't stop trying! <u>You are AWESOME</u>!

I once heard, "If your Dream doesn't scare you, it's NOT big enough!"

There is no one exactly like you and that's okay! God made us all a little different for a reason – to learn from each other. (We are all different, but the same in many ways – we're more alike than we are different!) A couple of rules for life: "Say what you mean and mean what you say."

Be Honest and forgiving, if you hold a grudge against anyone, you're only cheating yourself and giving away your own piece of mind. And most importantly, The Golden Rule, Treat others the way, you want to be treated! Love people and love yourselves! Take the time to appreciate the blue sky, green grass, clouds, animals, and each other. We live in a beautiful world.

(Little things matter.)

The many faces of BOB